Charles Davis, John Thomson

A description of the works of art forming the collection of Alfred de Rothschild

Rothschild

Vol. 1

Charles Davis, John Thomson

A description of the works of art forming the collection of Alfred de Rothschild
Vol. 1

ISBN/EAN: 9783337311001

Printed in Europe, USA, Canada, Australia, Japan

Cover: Foto ©Raphael Reischuk / pixelio.de

More available books at **www.hansebooks.com**

A

DESCRIPTION

OF THE

WORKS OF ART

FORMING THE COLLECTION OF

ALFRED DE ROTHSCHILD.

THE PHOTOGRAPHS BY J. THOMPSON, F.R.G.S.

VOLUME I.

PICTURES.

COMPILED BY CHARLES DAVIS,

147, NEW BOND STREET, LONDON.

1884.

PREFACE.

THE following pages contain a description of the Pictures and other Works of Art belonging to me in Seamore Place and at Halton.

The principal objects, and those which, needless to say, I most prize, I inherited from my dearly beloved father, and, in addition to the great pleasure which they afford me, they constantly remind me of his most perfect judgment and taste.

Where descriptions of pictures are given in inverted commas, they are taken from Smith's Catalogue Raisonné.

To Mr. Thomson, of Grosvenor Street, I am indebted for the accuracy of the illustrations, whilst to Mr. Davis I can never sufficiently express my acknowledgments for his care and attention in compiling these volumes.

ALFRED DE ROTHSCHILD.

July, 1884.

CONTENTS.

VOLUME I.

CONTENTS.

CONTENTS.

CONTENTS.

C. signifies painted on Canvas.

P. signifies painted on Panel.

VIEWS

OF THE

PRINCIPAL ROOMS

IN

SEAMORE PLACE.

PICTURES.

1.

MRS. BEAUFOY.
BY
GAINSBOROUGH.

THIS lady is represented standing in a nearly front view, with her head turned slightly to the right. She is attired in a yellow satin dress, trimmed with blue and ornamented with a lace frill and pearls; a light muslin scarf, one end of which she holds in her hand, falls gracefully over her right shoulder; her hair is decked with pearls. A richly wooded park forms the background.

Inscribed, " Mrs. Beaufoy—by Gainsborough."

———

7 ft. by 4 ft. 7½ in.   C.

2.

MISS ANGELO.

BY

SIR JOSHUA REYNOLDS.

REPRESENTED with her face towards the left; her hair is powdered, and one curl falls gracefully over her right shoulder. She wears a yellow dress, a light muslin fichu, and a large black hat with a feather. A crimson curtain forms the background.

————

2 ft. 6 in. by 2 ft. 1 in.   C.

3.

LADY PAULETT.

BY

ROMNEY.

THIS lady is represented seated on a couch, with her hands crossed and her left arm resting on a marble pedestal, on the front of which is a carved wreath. Her head is turned slightly to the right; her hair is powdered and falls in curls over her shoulders. She is attired in a white satin dress trimmed with twisted bands of pink ribbon, and a shawl is thrown lightly over her left arm. A wooded landscape forms the background.

———

4 ft. by 3 ft. 4 in.   C.

4.

Miss Tickell.

BY

Romney.

A HALF-LENGTH portrait in a nearly front view. The lady's head is turned slightly to the left; her hair is in ringlets on her forehead, and falls gracefully over her shoulders. She wears a large hat with feathers, and her dress, which is open in front, is of a light white material ; a broad band of silk encircles her waist.

————

2 ft. 5½ in. by 2 ft. ½ in.   C.

5.

LADY HAMILTON.

BY

ROMNEY.

THIS beautiful lady is seated on a crimson couch; she is clasping a book in her arms and her right elbow rests on a marble balustrade. Her eyes are raised, and she appears lost in meditation. Her attire consists of a rose-coloured dress with a dark overskirt, a white bodice, and a light scarf over her shoulders. From under a large hat, her luxuriant hair falls about her face and neck.

———

4 ft. 1 in. by 3 ft. 4 in.   C.

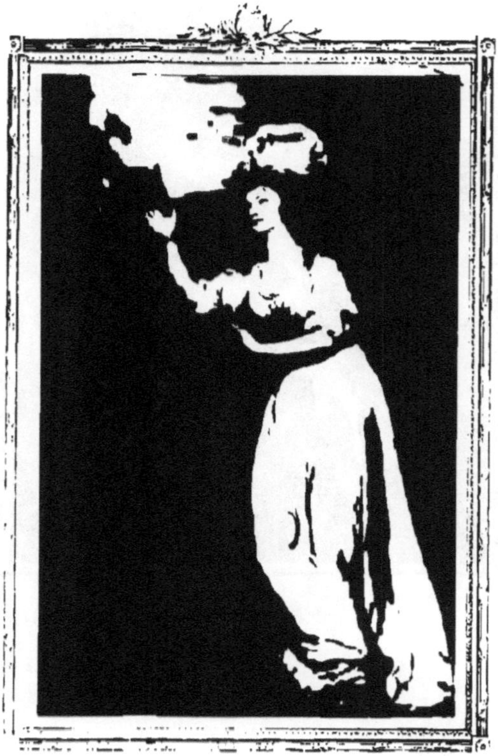

6.

Mrs. Webster, afterwards Lady Vassall Holland.

BY
Romney.

THIS lady is standing with her feet slightly crossed, and leaning against a square pedestal, on the front of which is an emblem of the sun; on her breast is a large ornament also emblematic of the sun. Her right arm rests on the pedestal, which she is touching with her left hand; her eyes and gestures are directed to the right, from which side falls a ray of light, and her attitude is that of contemplation. Her hair, which falls in curls over her shoulders, is adorned with a crown of white feathers. She wears a loose flowing white dress, with short sleeves.

———

7 ft. by 4 ft. 7½ in. C.

7.

PEASANTS RETURNING FROM MARKET.

BY

NICHOLAS BERGHEM.

" A HILLY and richly wooded scene, on the right of which are, a woman on a mule, and a man on foot, with cattle ; the former, wearing a blue skirt, is seen in a side view, and the latter is arranging her stirrup board ; behind is a mule heavily laden with packages : they appear to have passed a narrow stream, through which a herdsman is about to drive a cow. From hence the eye looks over an extent of broken ground, dotted with travellers, to some buildings situate near a river. The left of the picture is composed of masses of rock, among which grow freely a variety of trees and bushes. The appearance is that of a fine clear morning. A most charming work of the master."

2 ft. 3½ in. by 2 ft. 9 in.   C.

8.

THE MUSICAL PEASANTS.

BY

NICHOLAS BERGHEM.

" THE scene exhibits a hilly country, with a noble river extending over a great portion of the view, bounded by a succession of hills. On the right are, a young woman on a grey horse, and a youth on an ass; the former is singing from a ballad which she holds, while the latter accompanies her on the flute,—the sound of the instrument has caused his beast to bray: with them are a youth on foot, conducting two cows, four sheep, and a goat, the whole of which are passing a ford. The opposite side is composed of a clump of high trees, of scanty foliage, beyond which is a peasant on a mule, with a herd of cattle, also passing a river; both groups are receding from the spectator. A warm evening.

Signed and dated 1645."

———

2 ft. 4 in. by 2 ft. 9½ in.   P.

9.

A Landscape.

BY

Nicholas Berghem.

"A LANDSCAPE, exhibiting a mountainous country, with some lofty rocks on the right, surmounted by a tower, and fenced at their base by hewn stone-work. Upon the margin of a pond, on the same side, stands a woman, dressed in a yellow gown, a red petticoat, and a blue bodice, pointing to some object, and at the same time looking towards a peasant who is seated near her. Two cows, an ass, four sheep, and a dog, are distributed over the foreground. A clear and excellent work, of the choicest quality."

———

1 ft. 8 in. by 2 ft.   C.

10.

A View on a River in Holland.

BY

Albert Cuyp.

"A VIEW on a river in Holland during a severe frost. On the left and front are eighteen fishermen, most of whom have long poles, and are engaged forcing nets under the ice : several tubs to receive the fish are standing near them. On the opposite side is a sledge, with two persons in it, drawn by a grey horse. A number of figures skating, and otherways amusing themselves, are distributed over the scene. The church of Dort is seen in the distance."

1 ft. 9 in. by 2 ft. 10½ in. P.

11.

A View on the Banks of the Maes.

BY

Albert Cuyp.

"ON the left of the foreground are four cows, three of which are lying down, with their heads towards the herdsman, who is seated in the middle playing on a bagpipe; while a boy in a red jacket, and having a stick in his hand, stands by listening. A little way off, on the left, are two persons riding on asses laden with panniers, coming over a hill. The more distant scenery is composed of a river, on whose extreme banks are seen some buildings. The fervid heat of a summer's afternoon lends a delightful lustre to this charming production."

———

1 ft. 7 in. by 2 ft. 5 in.   P.

12.

Halt of Cavaliers at an Inn.

BY

Albert Cuyp.

" THREE gentlemen have just arrived at a country inn, and two of them have dismounted from grey and bay horses, which stand together with the reins attached to a tree; the third cavalier still remains on his steed, near which is one of the riders, seated on a form at the side of the house (only a small part of which is seen): he has a cane in his hand, his dog is by him, and a tankard and glass are within his reach.

The distance exhibits an open country, divided by a canal and diversified with bushy trees; and the whole scene is brilliantly illumined by the glowing tints of a summer's evening."

---

1 ft. 6 in. by 2 ft. 4½ in.   P.

13.

PORTRAIT OF A LADY.

BY

GERARD DOW.

"A LADY, elegantly dressed in a green silk corset, bordered with fur, seated, playing on a virginal, which is placed on a table covered with a Persian carpet; some music-books lie on the table, and a violoncello stands against it in front. The lady is represented sitting at a window, the curtain of which is drawn up on one side. A company of three persons and a servant waiting on them, are seen in the back of the room.

Descamps mentions this picture, which was then in the collection of the Maréchal d'Issenhein, 1754."

———

15½ in. by 12½ in.   P.

14.

A YOUNG WOMAN AT A WINDOW.

BY

GERARD DOW.

A YOUNG woman at a window, emptying water out of a brass milk-can; a pot of flowers and a piece of carpet are upon the sill, and at the side hangs a bird-cage. Near a window, at the back of the room, another woman is cutting a slice of bread for a boy.

———

1 ft. 3 in. by 1 ft.   P.

15.

Two Gentlemen Drinking.

BY

Peter de Hooge.

"TWO gentlemen, seated at table in the paved court of a house, enjoying their glass ; the nearest of these to the spectator, dressed in a suit of black velvet, is seated, with a large grey cloak over his knees; his companion, wearing a cuirass, sits on the farther side of the table, looking at the hostess, who stands by its side, drinking. She is dressed in a drab jacket, a scarlet skirt, and a blue apron; behind her is a child approaching with a pot of embers in her hands. An open door in a high wall at the extremity of the court, shows an adjacent garden. The tower of Utrecht church is seen on the opposite side. This is a clear and good example of the master."

———

2 ft. 2 in. by 1 ft. 10½ in.   C.

16.

FRUIT AND FLOWERS.
BY
JOHN VAN HUYSUM.

" A RICH variety of fruit, consisting of white and purple grapes, peaches, plums, and raspberries, tastefully mingled with a few flowers, the most conspicuous of which are the hollyhock and scarlet lychnis, and these conceal in part an elegant vase. This superlative performance may be distinguished from others by a drone fly. A bunch of hazel nuts, and a broken pomegranate hang on the left of the marble slab. A faint indication of a grove forms the background. Signed, and dated 1722."

———

2 ft. 7½ in. by 2 ft.   P.

17.

FLOWERS,

BY

JOHN VAN HUYSUM.

"A SPLENDID assemblage of flowers, consisting of roses, anemones, ranunculuses, hyacinths, tulips, &c., disposed in an elegant vase, adorned with a bas-relief of nymphs and cupids, placed on a Sienna marble table, on which are also a chaffinch's nest with four eggs in it, and a bunch of flowers, composed of a rosebud, honeysuckles, and convolvuluses. This estimable production is painted on a light ground. Signed, and dated 1722."

———

2 ft. 7½ in. by 2 ft.   P.

18.

LA FRAÎCHE MATINÉE.

BY

KAREL DU JARDIN.

"A VIEW in Italy, exhibited under the aspect of a fine clear morning. The country offers a hilly site, with a stream of water near the front, through which is passing a woman, dressed in a blue gown and a red skirt, holding up her clothes with both hands, and at the same time turning her head towards a shepherd, who sits on a bank in front, with his back to the spectator. An ass having on a pack-saddle, a sheep, a goat, and a calf, are also in the stream; beyond which is a long wall, enclosing two houses and a shrubbery. The distance terminates by receding mountains. This is a choice and estimable production. Signed, and dated 1657."

1 ft. 8 in. by 1 ft. 6 in.   C.

19.

Le Corset Bleu.

BY

Gabriel Metsu.

" A LADY, attired in a blue corset bordered with ermine, and a white satin skirt trimmed with gold lace, seated, with a music-book on her lap, a leaf of which she is about to turn over. A table, covered in part with a Persian carpet, is placed by her, on the farther side of which sits a gentleman tuning a guitar. A glass of wine stands on the table, and a little spaniel is in front. The elegance and taste displayed in the drawing, colouring, execution, and sentiment of this picture, render it a *bijou* of uncommon beauty and value."

----

1 ft. 4 in. by 11 in.   P.

20.

A Lady at her Toilet.

BY

Gaspar Netscher

"A LADY, of a pleasing countenance, and light hair, attired in a white satin robe and blue skirt, standing in nearly a front view, in the act of attaching a bracelet of pearls on her wrist; she is attended by a negro page, bearing a dish of fruit. Upon a table, covered with a Turkey carpet, are a looking-glass, and other objects, appertaining to the toilet. This is an exquisitely finished picture."

———

1 ft. 6½ in. by 1 ft. 2 in.   P.

21.

VERTUMNUS AND POMONA.

BY

GASPAR NETSCHER.

" THIS beautiful and highly-finished picture represents a young lady dressed
in white satin with a blue scarf over her left shoulder, seated, resting her left
arm on a marble table covered with a carpet, on which are some peaches, &c. She
holds in her hand a pruning-knife, and an apple is in her lap ; she appears listening to
the persuasions of a comely old lady, who stands leaning on her staff on the other side
of the table, dressed in a marone-coloured cloak, with a black scarf over her head. A
statue of Venus is behind, and two figures in niches are seen in a grove in the background."

---

19 in. by 15½ in.   P.

22.

THE PRINCESS ANN.

BY

GASPAR NETSCHER.

" PORTRAIT of the Princess Ann, daughter of James II., when about twenty
years of age, richly attired in an embroidered blue silk robe with full lace
sleeves, represented standing near a sculptured table, caressing a spaniel. A theorbo
and book are on the table. A shrubbery, adorned with statues, forms the background.
This exquisitely wrought picture is signed and dated 1683."

———

2 ft. 4½ in. by 2 ft. 11 in. C.

23.

LA TRICOTEUSE.

BY

GASPAR NETSCHER.

" **A** PRETTY young woman, dressed in a blue bodice, a tawny-yellow satin skirt, a white apron, and a black cap, seated at an arched window, knitting. A table, covered with a Turkey carpet, stands before her, on which is a basket containing balls of worsted. This is an elegant and highly-studied production."

———

11½ in. by 8¾ in. P.

24.

VILLAGERS DANCING AND REGALING.

BY

ADRIAN VAN OSTADE.

" THE cheerful scene is passing in front of some cottages occupying the right of the picture, one of which is distinguished by a vine growing luxuriantly over some trellis-work, and a fine clump of trees rises at the extremity of the houses. The dancers, consisting of two couples, occupy the centre of the foreground; one of the females, dressed in a blue gown and a purple skirt, is gaily footing it with a peasant, who holds his hat in his hand. Among the surrounding spectators interested in the passing scene are three boors, one of whom, wearing a purplish jacket and a red cap, sits on a form with a pipe in his hand; another is raising his replenished glass to the health of his companions; on the same side, but nearer the front, are two children playing with a terrier dog close to a cask and a stool. A social group of four persons, may also be noticed under the shade of the trellis-work, and in addition to these are an old man seated near a tilted cart with a jug in his hand, and the mirth-stirring fiddler mounted on a tub. The more distant scenery exhibits a continuation of the village. This most enchanting work of art is dated 1660."

———

1 ft. 4¾ in. by 1 ft. 10½ in. P.

25.

The Fruit Stall.

BY

Isaac van Ostade.

" A VIEW of some picturesque cottages, standing on the summit of a hill on the left, with an ascent of rustic stone steps to the top of it; a brick wall forms a fence to the embankment of the hill, and an archway of the same materials crosses a road, and abuts against the wall; at the side of which, and near the front, is an old woman, keeping a stall with fruit and vegetables; another woman stands with a basket on her arm, behind whom are two boys and a girl, at play; and upon the hill above her is a woman seated, spinning; a man, carrying a basket, is descending the steps; a pig-sty, and various rustic objects, are on the right side.

An excellent picture, painted in the artist's best time."

———

23 in. by 18 in.   P.

26.

The Water Mill.

BY

Paul Potter.

" THE view represents a hilly scene, with a meadow fore-ground, bounded by high banks, covered in part by bushes, and having an overshot water-mill placed on the right. Three cows, a calf, two goats, a kid, several lambs and sheep, and an ass, are variously distributed over the field; and a boy sits on a bank, on the farther side of it, watching them. In the distance is seen the tower of a château. The dewy freshness of early morning pervades the rural scene.

This carefully finished production is signed, and dated 1653."

———

1 ft. 10 in. by 2 ft.   C.

27.

A LANDSCAPE.

BY

JACOB RUYSDAEL.

A LANDSCAPE with oak and other trees. A river flowing through high banks forms a cascade in the foreground, in which is a fallen tree. In the centre of the picture, behind the river, is a castle.

---

1 ft. 4 in. by 2 ft. 1 in.   C.

28

A Village Wedding.

BY

Jan Steen.

"NUMEROUS persons are assembled in a short street of a Dutch town, to accompany the bride on her arrival from church, while the bridegroom, wearing a scarlet cap and a bright grey dress, and with a smiling countenance, is seen descending the steps of a house on the right, to receive and welcome her; the merry music of a bagpiper and fiddler enlivens the scene. Behind the bride, and on the steps of a door, is a droll fellow enjoying the fun; near him stands a boy; and in front are a cock, a hen, and other objects."

———

1 ft. 8 in. by 1 ft. 6½ in.　P.

29

THE MARRIAGE OF TENIERS.

BY

DAVID TENIERS.

" THE scene represents a pleasure-garden, adorned with rows of trees, and refreshed by a fountain. The artist and his lovely bride are being conducted to their château by a splendid cortége, consisting of upwards of twenty persons of distinction, accompanied by a musician playing on a guitar, and attended by youths preparing refreshments. The beauty of a fine summer's day adds life and gaiety to the joyous event. Dated 1651.

This picture possesses all the attractive qualities peculiar to the master—freedom and lightness of pencilling, a sweet and silvery tone of colouring, and a composition of peculiar interest and beauty."

———

2 ft. 3 in. by 2 ft. 10 in.   P.

30.

A Village Feast.

BY

David Teniers.

"THE festive scene, composed of about seventy persons, is represented as passing in the enclosed court of a guinguette; the house stands on the left, with a cottage adjoining it. In the centre of the court are three women and two men dancing, in a ring, to the music of a bagpipe, played by a man standing under a lofty tree. On the left, in front, is a company of thirteen persons, disposed round a table; amongst whom is a man in a yellow jacket, with his arm round a woman's neck. On the farther side of the table are the landlord and a woman, the former standing at the door of the house, and the latter just within it; beyond these is a large company regaling under a penthouse, and others in chat near it. On the opposite side, and front, are eight figures; amongst whom is a woman endeavouring to raise a drunken man; at her side is a boor inviting a woman to dance; a little retired from these are a number of peasants, near the paling of the court, and one being led out of the door by two men. A variety of culinary utensils lie on the foreground; a village and the spire of a church are seen in the distance.

This excellent production offers an example of the artist's most spirited and fascinating style of handling, aided by a sparkling brilliancy of colouring, which gives life and movement to the numerous groups which compose it. The date of it, 1646, is on a flag which flies from a window of the house."

———

1 ft. 10½ in. by 2 ft. 6½ in.　P.

31.

PEASANTS DANCING.

BY

DAVID TENIERS.

THE scene represents a number of peasants collected outside a country inn ; some of them are seated round a table regaling themselves. The principal figures are a man and a woman, who are dancing to the strains of a bagpipe played by a man standing on a cask. In the foreground is an old man leaning on a staff, watching the dancing, and behind him is a seat on which stand a jug and a glass.

———

10 in. by 1 ft. 1½ in.   P.

32.

A Card Party.

Gerard Terburg.

" A CARD party, composed of two ladies and a gentleman. One of the former, dressed in a rich white satin robe with a rose-coloured body, and a fur tippet, is seated, with her back to the spectator, holding her cards down in her lap: her adversary, attired in a blue satin robe with a silver-grey body, both of which are embroidered with gold, sits on the opposite side in a front view, looking at her cards ; and the gentleman, habited in the elegant costume of the period, sits on her right, directing her in the game. The table is covered with a Turkey carpet, and a bottle and a silver salver are on it. This is a clear and most delightful production."

———

1 ft. 6 in. by 1 ft. 2½ in.   C. (on panel).

33.

A LADY SINGING.
BY
GERARD TERBURG.

" THE subject is composed of a young lady and a gentleman; the former, attired in a blue jacket bordered with ermine, and a white satin petticoat, is seated on the right, seen in a front view, playing on a theorbo, and accompanying the air with her voice; her eyes at the same time are directed to the cavalier, who sits on a table, listening to the music: upon the table, which is covered with a Turkey carpet, are a music-book and a watch."

———

1 ft. 4 in. by 1 ft. 2 in.   P.

34.

VIEW OF A CHÂTEAU.

BY

JOHN VANDER HEYDEN.

" VIEW of a handsome Château of the Roman style of architecture, built of stone, and enclosed by a brick wall, surmounted by a stone balustrade adjoining a noble gate of entrance of a corresponding style. On the opposite side is a cluster of trees, concealing in part, a building, apparently the porter's lodge. The pencil of A. V. Velde has given additional interest and value to this exquisitely finished picture, by the introduction of a variety of figures, of which the principal are a gentleman coming from the gate, followed by a domestic, and preceded by three dogs; a poor woman, with a child at her back, awaits his approach. On the farther side of the gate sits a gentleman on a fragment of architecture, putting a collar on a dog; two other dogs lie near him. A fine morning."

---

1 ft. 7½ in. by 2 ft. 3 in. P.

35.

Rendez-vous de Chasse.
BY
Adrian Vander Velde.

"A HUNTING party assembled on a paved terrace adjacent to some noble mansion, and in the precincts of a woody park. A stone pedestal, surmounted by a statue of Hercules, is on the right, from whence a lady and gentleman, elegantly habited, are advancing towards a beautiful white palfrey, caparisoned with a blue velvet saddle and housings, and held by a page in a scarlet dress. A little retired from these is a huntsman on a chestnut horse, blowing his horn, and still farther are a pack of hounds and several huntsmen. Beyond the lady and gentleman are seen the equipages of the family, drawn by grey horses; and close to the front are two venerable pilgrims asking charity. Signed, and dated 1662.

The elegance of the figures, the beautiful symmetry of the horses, and the number and variety of the dogs, render this a most interesting example of the master."

———

1 ft. 6¾ in. by 2 ft.   C.

36.

A Landscape under the aspect of Summer,
by
Adrian Vander Velde.

"THE country is intersected by a road on the left, passing at the base of a sandy bank, on which are two trees. A sportsman, with a gun in his hand and a hare at his back, is on the road ; and a little farther is a second gentleman on a grey horse, of whom a woman is begging. Beyond the latter are a boy and a girl reposing. This is a delightful specimen of art. Dated 1665."

10 in. by ⨉ in. P.

37.

The Piping Herdsman.
by
Adrian Vander Velde.

"THE view offers a pleasing woody scene, with a fountain in front, adorned with a sculptured vase, at the foot of which are seated a herdsman and a woman. The former is playing on a pipe, and the latter is reclining on his knees, listening to the music. A cow, a sheep, and two lambs, are browsing near them ; and upon a hill in the distance is the ruin of a building. Signed, and dated 1671."

10 in. by 1 ft. 3 in. P.

38.

VIEW ON THE DUTCH COAST.

BY

WILLIAM VANDER VELDE.

" VIEW on the Dutch coast during a fine calm morning. The composition offers, in the centre, a boat, containing three men and two large fishing baskets; a little retired from this is a merchant ship, with her sails hanging loosely on the yards; two small boats lie alongside of her, and over her stern are seen three fishing smacks. On the opposite side is a coaster, approaching under main and foresails, and considerably remote from this are a frigate and two small vessels."

---

1 ft. 3 in. by 1 ft. 8 in.   C.

39.

La Fontaine de Vénus.

BY

Philip Wouwermans.

" A LANDSCAPE, with a handsome fountain on the right, composed of a female
with cupids; near which is a sporting party, consisting of a lady and two
gentlemen, who have stopped to refresh themselves; one of the gentlemen has just
dismounted from a fine piebald horse, and is assisting the lady to alight; at a little
distance from this group, and near the fountain, is a man with a horse, laden with a fine
stag; two couples of dogs, and a horse, are drinking at the fountain, and a dog lies
near a dead hare, in front, &c., &c."

———

15 in. by 20 in.   P.

40.

Travellers Halting at a House.

BY

Philip Wouwermans.

"TRAVELLERS halting at an old house, situate on the left of the picture. One of them is on a fine piebald horse; the other, wearing a red cap, appears to be about to mount a bay horse: a little beyond these is a groom, riding a restive grey steed down the bank of a river, in which two boys are bathing, and two others are preparing to enter the stream: two boys are also seen on a wall, near the door of the house. On the opposite side are two dogs quarrelling; one of them is held by a boy. Painted in the latter time of the artist; clear and beautiful in tone."

---

1 ft. 4 in. by 1 ft. 8½ in.   P.

41.

A Hawking Party.

BY

Philip Wouwermans.

"A LANDSCAPE with a party of ladies and gentlemen on horseback, passing a ford, followed by attendants with dogs, amongst whom is a huntsman on a fine white horse, preceded by a lady wearing a black cap decked with feathers, on a horse richly caparisoned ; the landscape is varied with hills and dales, and illumined by a fine clear sky.

This picture is truly one of the artist's *chefs-d'œuvre :* it is clear and luminous, and appears to have been painted about the time that he adopted his third manner."

———

21 in. by 27 in.   C.

42.

A Hawking Party.

BY

Philip Wouwermans.

"A HAWKING party, consisting of a lady and two gentlemen on horseback, the former is mounted on a beautiful white palfrey, and one of the latter is casting up the lure to the hawks; these are accompanied by their attendants and dogs; others belonging to the company are seen in the distance: the landscape offers an open country, varied by gentle hills, represented under the aspect of an overcast sky, indicating wind and rain."

The companion to the last picture.

———

21 in. by 27 in.   C.

43

SOLDIERS GAMBLING.

BY

PHILIP WOUWERMANS.

" A LANDSCAPE, exhibiting a hilly country, on the foreground of which are three soldiers and a sportsman, grouped around a drum, gambling. The latter person has a dog and a gun by his side; one of the former appears to have dismounted from a white horse, and is standing behind his steed, in the rear of which are two other horses. A woman, with a child in her arms, accompanied by a man, are close to the right; and on the opposite side is a cavalier on horseback, going towards a horse and cart. Some tents and military are seen on a distant hill.

This excellent picture was painted in the artist's latter period."

———

1 ft. 2 in. by 1 ft. 4 in.   P.

44.

A Halt of Huntsmen.
BY
Philip Wouwermans.

" THE view exhibits a hilly landscape with a ruin on the left, composed of an arch, abutting against a pedestal, surmounted by the statue of a warrior. In the foreground are a lady in a blue habit (seated), and a gentleman by her side, offering her a cup of drink; behind these is a page, holding a brown horse and a fine grey palfrey: near them are two dogs and a dead stag: towards the ruin are two huntsmen, one of whom is seated on the ground, the other is mounted on a bay horse. A fountain, adorned with sea-horses, at which a sportsman is filling a bottle, is close to the right side of the picture, and completes the composition of this exquisite little gem."

---

13 in. by 19 in.   P.

45.

HAWKING PARTY.

BY

J. WYNANTS.

"THE view represents a country of a highly picturesque character, composed, on the right, of a decayed elm standing on a broken bank, and a little beyond it is an enclosed meadow, in which are an ox and a horse; the view is then bounded by a wood. Upon a winding road, which leads from the front and along the skirts of the wood, is a falconer carrying a hoop of hawks, followed by two dogs; and a little retired from him is a second sportsman, sitting by the side of the road, with two dogs near him : considerably beyond these is a gentleman on a dun-coloured horse, accompanied by a lady on a grey one, followed by dogs. The left of the view offers a valley of considerable extent, agreeably diversified ; and the aspect of a fine morning lends a charm to the scene. The figures are admirably introduced by Lingelbach."

Dated, 1661.

1 ft. 9 in. by 2 ft. 2 in.   C.

46.

THE BIRTH AND TRIUMPH OF VENUS.

BY

FRANÇOIS BOUCHER.

A N oval picture comprising fourteen figures. In the centre, the lovely goddess is represented reclining on a blue couch, which is floating on the waves; her head is turned towards the spectator, and she is clasping a dove; her hair is decorated with a pink ribbon. At her feet are two nymphs presenting some pearls and coral on a shell, and in front three cupids are disporting themselves on the backs of two dolphins; there are also two tritons in the water, one of whom is blowing a trumpet to soothe the waves. In the light blue sky are two cupids supporting some drapery, a third holding a bow and arrow, and a fourth with a garland of flowers.

Signed, F. Boucher, 1743.

———

3 ft. 4 in. by 2 ft. 10 in.   C.

47.

THE TOILET OF VENUS.

BY

FRANÇOIS BOUCHER.

THE goddess is reposing on some blue drapery, and a nymph behind her is decking her hair with pearls, which are handed by two other nymphs from a casket on a gilt table, on which Venus is resting her left arm. Her face is turned to the spectator, and she appears lost in thought. A cupid is binding her foot with a pink ribbon, whilst three others support a mirror in which her face is reflected in profile; above them is a cupid holding a dove, and another supporting in the air the rose-coloured curtain, which forms part of the background. On the ground, which is strewn with flowers, are a gilt ewer and a silver salver; the car of the goddess, partly hidden by clouds, is on the right.

Signed, F. Boucher, 1743.

———

3 ft. 4 in. by 2 ft. 10½ in.   C.

48.

CUPID DISARMED BY VENUS.

BY

FRANÇOIS BOUCHER.

IN the centre, Venus is represented supported on the clouds. In her left hand is one of Cupid's arrows, and with her right she holds aloft a quiver full of arrows, which Cupid is vainly endeavouring to recover. Her hair is decked with pearls, and a light drapery falls gracefully over her arms. Behind is her car, and at her feet two white doves.

Signed, F. Boucher.

---

3 ft. 2 in. by 2 ft. 8¼ in.   C.

49.

VENUS CARESSING CUPID.

BY

FRANÇOIS BOUCHER.

THE goddess is represented reposing on rose-coloured drapery, amidst the clouds. Her right arm encircles a charming cupid, into whose eyes she is tenderly gazing; her hair is decked with pearls, and in her left hand is a ribbon by which she holds captive two doves at her feet. To the right is a table with a gilt ewer upon it.

---

3 ft. 2 in. by 2 ft. 8½ in.   C.

50.

Mademoiselle Duthé.

BY

Drouais.

A THREE-QUARTER portrait of this young lady, who is leaning on a velvet cushion placed on a stone balustrade; in front of the cushion, which is bordered with gold lace, are a book and a work-bag. Her arms are crossed, and in her right hand she holds a fan. She wears a grey satin dress trimmed with flowers, with a square open body and short sleeves with lace ruffles; round her neck is a lace fichu. A landscape forms the background.

———

4 ft. 2 in. by 3 ft.   C.

51.

THE KISS SENT.
BY
GREUZE.

"A HANDSOME young lady, represented in nearly a front view, standing at a window, looking tenderly at some distant object, and at the same time raising one hand to her lips; the other hand holds a letter on the sill; her head gracefully inclines on one side, and her flaxen hair is decked with flowers. A curtain is on either side of the window, and a pot of flowers stands on the sill. Engraved in a decorated oval, under the title of 'La Voluptueuse, by Gaillard.'"

———

3 ft. by 2 ft. 6 in.   C.

52.

MEDITATING OVER THE CONTENTS OF A LETTER.
BY
GREUZE.

"A YOUNG woman in her night clothes, seated, meditating over the contents of a letter."

2 ft. 2 in. by 1 ft. 8 in.   C.

53.

PORTRAIT OF A YOUNG GIRL.
BY
GREUZE.

THE bust of a girl of fair complexion, resting her head pensively on her right hand. Her hair is light and plaited on the top; falling from her shoulders is a loose violet garment.

---

1 ft. 4 in. by 1 ft. ½ in.   C.

54.

PORTRAIT OF A BOY.

BY

GREUZE.

THE bust of a boy with curly flaxen hair, attired in a grey vest with a large white frilled collar. He is represented in a nearly front view with his eyes directed towards the right.

———

1 ft. 3½ in. by 1 ft. ¼ in.   C.

55.

A Pastoral Scene

BY

Huet.

A SMALL oval picture of a shepherd and shepherdess seated under a tree in a
field of ripe corn. The shepherd is twining a garland of roses round his companion, whose right hand is on his shoulder; in her left hand the shepherdess holds a
blue ribbon, which is tied round the neck of a lamb at her feet.

6 in. by 9 in.   C.

56.

EARTH.

BY

LANCRET.

A PARTY of ladies and gentlemen in a garden. On the right is a tree laden with fruit, which a young man on a ladder is gathering, and throwing to a girl, who is holding out her dress to receive it; in front of the tree are two men, one digging, the other watering the flowers. To the left, three girls are examining the fruit which has been gathered, and behind them is a youth presenting a nosegay to the lady at his side. In the background is a terrace ornamented with sculpture and a fountain.

1 ft. 3½ in. by 1 ft.   C.

57.

WATER.

BY

LANCRET.

A SCENE on the bank of a river. In the centre of the picture, a man in a red coat is netting fish, and on the edge of the bank a girl is fishing with a rod. In the foreground is a boy with bare arms and legs, kneeling on the grass and placing some fish in the extended apron of the girl by his side, whilst behind them, near a tree, a man appears to be watching the proceedings. In the background are a farmhouse and a water-mill.

1 ft. 4½ in. by 1 ft. 1 in.   C.

58.

Spring.

by

Lanchet.

A GIRL., holding a basket of bright-coloured flowers, is gazing into the eyes of the youth at her side, who has placed his left arm round her shoulder. Behind them a girl appears more intent on watching the young couple than attending to the flowers which she is watering. On the left of the picture is a sculptured fountain, from which the water flows freely.

———

10½ in. by 1 ft. 2 in.   P.

59.

Winter.

by

Lancret.

IN the centre of the picture a young man is skating, watched by a maiden, who is having her skates fixed by a youth kneeling on the bank. In the background are a house and some trees.

———

10½ in. by 1 ft. 2 in.   P.

60.

THE MINUET.
BY
LANCRET.

A PARTY of ladies and gentlemen dispersed amidst the glades of a wooded garden. Near a fountain, embellished with sculptured nymphs supporting a triton, is a young lady elegantly attired, dancing the minuet with a youth, to the accompaniment of a musician on the left; behind them are six ladies and gentlemen looking on; in the foreground a young man, seated on the grass, is gazing at two ladies on the extreme right, who are watching the dancers.

An oval picture.

---

1 ft. 11 in. by 2 ft. 3 in.   C.

61.

THE PLEASURE BARGE.

BY

PATER.

CLOSE to the bank of a winding river a pleasure-barge is moored, covered with a canopy elegantly draped and decked with festoons of flowers. Several ladies and gentlemen are seated on the barge, and under the canopy a lady is standing, in conversation with her cavalier; behind them two girls are looking at a lady and her companion seated on the grass, who are also watched by a couple stepping on to the landing-board of the barge. To the right is a party of ladies and gentlemen reclining on the bank, and a figure robed in white is kneeling in the water.

In the distance are a châlet and a range of mountains.

—— ——

2 ft. 1 in. by 2 ft. 7¼ in.   C.

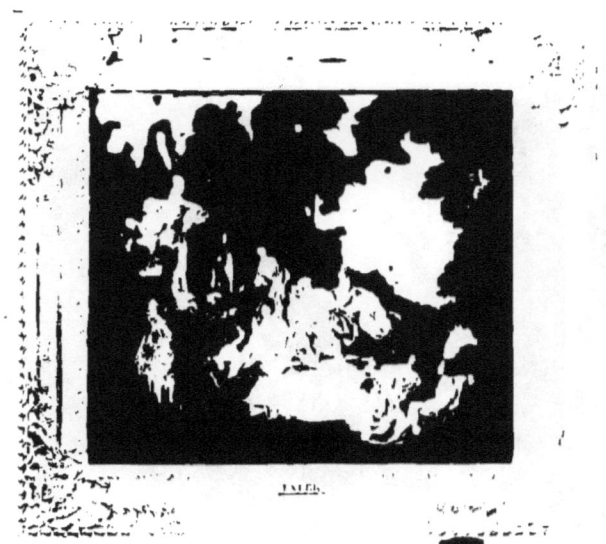

62.

LE BAIN.

BY

PATER.

THE scene represents two groups of female bathers beside a small pool, which is supplied by a fountain surmounted by a river deity; the water overflows from a shell held by two dolphins. A lady in a blue dress is leaning against the fountain and listening to the conversation of a gentleman at her side; they are closely observed by two of the bathers seated on the ground. On the bank to the right are a lady and a gentleman.

———

1 ft. 10 in. by 2 ft. 2 in.   C.

63.

THE SWING.

BY

PATER.

ON the left of the picture a young lady is seated in a swing, which is set in motion by a young man in the foreground dressed in crimson, assisted by another behind her; a third, recumbent on the grass, is watching them, in which occupation a gentleman on the right, holding a musical instrument, and the two girls near him, are also engaged. In the centre, a lady is having her hair decked with flowers by a gentleman, who takes them from the apron of a girl at his side; to their left a lady with a fan is seated, talking to her companion, whilst a girl behind them appears to follow the conversation. The background is formed by a mound and a clump of trees amidst which is a statue, and in the distance is a châlet.

—

1 ft. 10 in. by 2 ft. 1 in.   C.

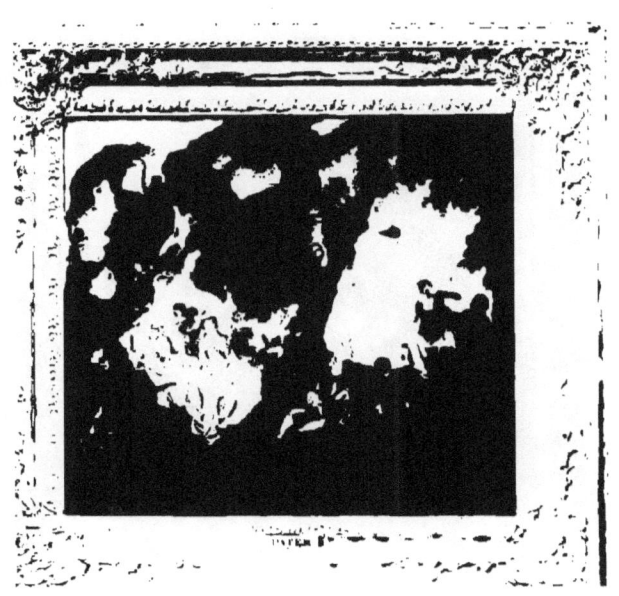

64.

LE REPOS DANS LE PARC.

BY

PATER.

A NUMBER of ladies and gentlemen wearing bright-coloured costumes are resting in a wooded park, some regaling themselves with wine handed by an attendant in Oriental costume, and others engaged in conversation. In the foreground a couple with their hands crossed, are dancing a minuet to the strains of a bagpipe played by an old man, accompanied by a youth on the violin. On the extreme right a little girl is playing with a dog.

---

1 ft. 10 in. by 2 ft. 1½ in. C.

65.

PLAISIRS CHAMPÊTRES.

BY

PATER.

IN a richly-wooded park, near a fountain composed of sculptured boys and dolphins, is a group of six ladies and gentlemen; the young lady seated in the centre is looking at a bird's nest held by the gentleman at her side. In the foreground, on the left, a lady and a youth are seated on the grass, weaving garlands of flowers. On the right a youth is gathering flowers, and throwing them into the apron of the girl at his side; another girl, seated on the grass, with her back to the spectator, is leaning against a basket of flowers. In the distance is a lake, with three figures on its bank, and beyond are a châlet and a range of mountains.

—

1 ft. 9½ in. by 2 ft. 1 in.   C.

66.

LA DANSE.

BY

PATER.

A PARTY of ladies and gentlemen assembled in a garden embellished with sculpture. Towards the left a lady and gentleman are dancing the minuet, to the accompaniment of the musicians on the right, and near the centre of the picture are others also dancing. A couple seated in the foreground are engaged in earnest conversation. Beneath a statue on the left is a young man offering some flowers to a lady, and near to them is a little girl playing with a dog. In the distance is a river with a village and châlets on its banks.

————

1 ft. 1½ in. by 1 ft. 6 in.   P.

67.

PEACE.

BY

PATER.

OUTSIDE of a tent, under which a number of soldiers are carousing, is a young lady seated on the grass, resisting the advances of a man whose arm is passed round her waist; on their left is a woman with a child in her arms, and in front a man lying on the ground. On the right of the picture are a lady and gentleman in conversation, and a girl, who appears to be listening. In the distance are tents, and several persons reclining on the grass. A hilly landscape, interspersed with houses and cottages, forms the background. Pervading the whole is an air of security, emblematic of peace.

---

11 in. by 1 ft 4½ in.   P.

68.

WAR.

BY

PATER.

IN the centre of the picture is a soldier with his arm round the waist of a young woman whose horse has fallen to the ground; they are anxiously watched by a peasant woman on a pony in the rear; near them is a group of peasants who seem afraid to interfere. A party of soldiers can be seen in the distance, defiling with their pack animals through the pass on the right. The scene presents an animated appearance, and seems to indicate a sudden order to change quarters; the details are emblematic of war.

---

11 in. by 1 ft. 4½ in.   P.

69.

LES AMANTS HEUREUX.

BY

PATER.

IN a garden embellished with sculpture, a lady is seated listening to the declarations of a cavalier by her side, and behind them stands a young man dressed in a loose red cloak, apparently smiling at the conversation. On their left, a lady in a blue dress is being assisted to rise by a youth. On the right a girl and two children are playing with some flowers. In the foreground is a spaniel stepping into a pool. In the distance are houses and a range of mountains.

---

1 ft. 5½ in. by 1 ft. 8½ in.   P.

Van Blakenberghe.

THE plates represent four of a series of six Gouache paintings; the description of the other two will be found at the end of this volume, Nos. 195—196.

70.

A Village Fray.

ON the left is a tavern, in front of which are men and women drinking round a table. Near to them an officer is endeavouring to draw his sword, but is restrained by a man and woman. Some distance behind them two men are fighting, surrounded by a crowd of villagers with raised hands and uplifted sticks; a number of peasants, coming from a church in the background, are watching the fray. In the distance is a river with boats upon it.

———

8¼ in. by 10½ in.

71.

THE VILLAGE MARRIAGE.

IN front of a tent are peasants regaling, while a bride is dancing with her bridegroom, to the music played by some men in their rear. On the right an officer watches the festivities, which are explained to him by a woman at his side; a mounted black servant holds his horse. In the distance a string of carts is approaching under the escort of two mounted soldiers; on the right are houses with mountains beyond.

7½ in. by 10½ in.

72.

PEASANTS DRINKING.

ON the right, an intoxicated peasant is being led away by a man and a woman, followed by a child ; near them a woman appears to be calling the attention of a man at her side to the delinquent, and behind, two women are endeavouring to rouse another man asleep on the ground. On the left is an inn, with a table outside, and peasants drinking and dancing ; behind them are two women surrounded by a crowd. In the distance is a wooded landscape, with numerous houses, figures and cattle.

8 in. by 10½ in.

73.

A WINTER SCENE.

A FROZEN river with houses and a castle on its banks ; near the centre a lady is having her skates fixed on by a man, and to her left is a gentleman with his hat under his arm, talking to another lady by his side ; scattered about are peasants going to market, people skating and sleighing, boys spinning tops and amusing themselves in various ways. In the distance is a large town and a range of mountains.

7¼ in. by 10¼ in.

74.

LA CASCADE.

BY

WATTEAU.

IN a garden shaded by tall trees a lady in a yellow dress is standing with a gentleman at her side. To their right is a large marble fountain composed of dolphins supporting a basin, on which three boys are holding a goat, from the mouth of which the water flows. Another couple half hidden by the foliage, is seen beneath the trees.

2 ft. 3 in. by 1 ft. 11 in. C.

75.

L'Accordée du Village.

BY

Watteau.

THE interest of this picture is centred in a bride and bridegroom, who are seated behind a table on which lies the marriage contract. The ceremony is being witnessed by a number of persons, and a priest holds a pen, in readiness for the signatures. Several couples are dancing to the music of two players seated on the left. In the foreground, on the right, are three little girls, one playing with a dog. The scene is represented in the grounds of a castle, which towers above the assembled party; on the right, in the distance, is a landscape with a village.

———

1 ft. 9½ in. by 2 ft. 3 in.   C.

76.

LA SÉRÉNADE ITALIENNE.

BY

WATTEAU.

A GROUP of six figures. A young lady is seated, listening to the music of four serenaders dressed in various costumes, two of whom are playing musical instruments; behind them a young man is looking on, and to the right, a little dog is stepping through the thick foliage which forms the background.

---

1 ft. 2 in. by 11 in.   P.

77.

HEUREUX AGE.

BY

WATTEAU.

SEATED on a low stone wall, in the centre of the picture, is a little boy; on his left a little girl is standing in the foreground with a bat under her arm, and another on his right, with folded hands, is seated on the grass; behind the wall are two more children.

— ·· —

7½ in. by 9½ in.   P.

78.

Portrait of Madame Elizabeth.

A FULL-LENGTH portrait of this lady standing with one foot lightly crossed over the other, and leaning, with her arms folded, against a marble pedestal, over which her shawl is thrown. She is looking at two white doves on the branch of a tree on the right. Her flaxen hair, adorned with ribbons, hangs in ringlets about her neck. Her white dress falls in graceful folds, a yellow silk scarf encircles her waist, and a small band of the same colour is round her arm. Behind her is a tree, and in the distance on the right a wooded landscape with a lake.

— · —

7 ft. by 4 ft 7½ in.   C.

79.

THE MAGDALEN.

BY

DOMENICHINO.

THE Magdalen is here represented facing the spectator, and pensively gazing upwards. Her hands are joined, and her left arm is resting on a pedestal. She wears a red dress, over which is a loose blue garment.

———

2 ft. 8 in. by 2 ft.   C.

80.

LUCRETIA.

BY

GUIDO RENI.

LUCRETIA is represented clasping in her right hand a dagger, which she has just plunged into her bosom. Her face is turned towards the left, and she is looking upwards. Her whole expression is that of anguish; her left hand is raised and appears to indicate her suffering. A loose blue garment and a yellow scarf are draped over her shoulders. A pink curtain forms the background.

———

2 ft. 8 in. by 2 ft. 2 in.   C.

80*.

Miss Ridge.

BY

Sir Joshua Reynolds.

THIS lady is represented in a front view, resting her left arm on a stone balustrade; her hair is decked with a blue ribbon, and a narrow band of velvet encircles her neck.

She wears a white dress trimmed with yellow, open in front. Her bodice is adorned with a blue silk bow, and a sash of the same colour is round her waist. Foliage forms the background.

28⅞ in. by 24½ in.

DESCRIPTION OF PICTURES NOT
ILLUSTRATED.

(

DESCRIPTION OF PICTURES NOT ILLUSTRATED.

195.

A River Scene.
BY
Van Blarenberghe.

THE scene represents a broad river, near which is a manor house, surrounded by a moat, and approached by a drawbridge. By the bank are a lady and gentleman in a carriage, who are saluted by a lame beggar and by two peasants leading a donkey. On the river is a large barge with a man and woman seated under an awning; two other figures are near the bow, and a man is climbing into the barge from a boat alongside. Beyond is a ferry-boat carrying men, women, and two horses; others are waiting on the banks for its return. In the far distance is a range of mountains.

9¼ in. by 11⅜ in.

196.

The Ferry.
BY
Van Blarenberghe.

NEAR the bank of a wide river is a ferry boat, into which a lady and gentleman are entering, followed by a servant carrying a basket of fruit. On the right are a gentleman and lady on horseback, in conversation; they are attended by a servant, and the lady's horse is in the water. Behind them is a barge decorated with flags, with several men and women on board. Outside an inn on the right are country people drinking.

9 in. by 11¼ in.

197.

Autumn.

by

François Boucher.

BY the side of a cornfield a cupid is asleep on a sheaf of corn near some rocks; his quiver full of arrows is on the ground near him, and another cupid is tickling him with an ear of wheat. Behind are two boys, one holding a sickle, and the other, with his back turned to the spectator, binding up a sheaf of corn.

3 ft. by 3 ft. 2 in. C.

198.

A Portrait of a Lady.

by

Drouais.

THIS lady is seated in a chair, holding a white spaniel on her lap. She wears a rich silk dress, open in front, with lace sleeves, and also a loose cloak of a rich gold brocaded material trimmed with dark fur. Her hair is powdered, and a double row of pearls encircles her neck.

2 ft. 7 in. by 2 ft. 1 in. C.

199.

The Girl and Spaniel.

by

Greuze.

A PORTRAIT of a child with brown hair, in a white dress lined with pink, and wearing a white kerchief on her head. Her body is turned to the left, and a light black scarf is thrown carelessly round her. In her arms she holds a small spaniel.

1 ft. 5¾ in. by 1 ft. 1½ in. C.

200.

A PORTRAIT OF A LADY.

BY

GREUZE.

AN oval portrait of a young woman seated in an arm-chair, her body turned to the right, with her left elbow resting on a cushion, and her hand lightly touching her neck. Her hat is decorated with a pink rose and white feathers; she wears a grey satin dress trimmed with gold fringe, and a large lace collar.

2 ft. 4 in. by 1 ft. 9½ in. C.

201.

THE SWING.

BY

LANCRET.

A GIRL, in a light pink dress with blue bodice, is seated in a swing suspended from the branch of a tree. A young man, standing in the foreground, is swinging her by means of a rope. In the background is a wooded park.

1 ft. 10½ in. by 1 ft. 6½ in. C.

202.

LA DANSE.

BY

LANCRET.

A LADY, dressed in a rose-coloured skirt and blue bodice, is dancing with a cavalier, whilst behind them a party of ladies and gentlemen are playing an accompaniment on various musical instruments. In the background are trees, through which the sky is seen.

11 in. by 8½ in.   C.

203.

THE SLEEPING SHEPHERDESS.

BY

LANCRET.

A LADY and three gentlemen are standing near a girl who is asleep under a tree. The gentleman on the left is taking away her crook, whilst the one on the right motions him not to awake the sleeper. The background is formed by trees through which the sky is seen.

204.

SUMMER.

BY

LARGILLIÈRE.

SUMMER is allegorically represented as a young woman with light hair, her body slightly turned to the right, holding with both hands a garland of roses and other flowers. On her wrists are pearl bracelets, and she wears a light-blue garment, thrown loosely over her right shoulder.

2 ft. 4 in. by 1 ft. 10 in.   C.

205.

LE CONCERT DE FAMILLE,
BY
PATER.

A GROUP of eight figures in the foreground of a landscape; some are playing whilst others are listening to the music. A page is bringing refreshments, and to the left a young man and a lady are seated on the grass. There is a marble statuette in the background.

8 in. by 11 in. P.

206.

LA CONVERSATION.
BY
WATTEAU.

IN a wooded park three ladies are seated on the grass, talking to a youth. To the right a couple are similarly engaged, as also are another couple standing close to a marble statue.

8 in. by 12 in. P.

207.

A LANDSCAPE,
BY
ALBERT CUYP.

IN the front of a sloping meadow a woman, dressed in a scarlet jacket with white sleeves, and a blue apron, is milking a cow. There are three other cows, two of which are lying down. An evening effect.

1 ft. 3 in. by 1 ft. 1½ in. P.

208.

A LANDSCAPE.

BY

HOBBEMA.

TO the right two men are walking along a path. Between the branches of the trees which meet in the centre of the picture can be seen a river, with three persons walking on the bank; there are farmhouses in the distance. Some fallen trees cover part of the foreground, and half hidden by the foliage on the right are the spires of a church On the left is a clear blue sky.

1 ft. 9¼ in. by 2 ft. 3¼ in.   C.

209

A BOAR HUNT.

BY

SNYDERS.

TO the left of the picture is a large boar chased by hounds, four of which are close to it. The infuriated animal, which has been seized by the ear by one of the pack, has overturned another of its assailants. In the foreground are eight of the hounds, some in a stream and some on the banks, also engaged in the pursuit. An open landscape forms the background.

6 ft. 10 in. by 11 ft. 1 in.   C.

210.

INTERIOR OF A FARM HOUSE.

BY

DAVID TENIERS.

ON the left seven peasants are grouped round a fire-place, some sitting, others standing. In the centre a man has just entered by an open doorway, through which a bright ray of light falls ; to the right another man is mounting a ladder leading to a loft. In the foreground is a dog, and near it are a bench and a wine-jug. In the background are kitchen utensils, and some fowls feeding.

———

1 ft. 5 in. by 1 ft. 10 in. P.

211.

INTERIOR OF A PICTURE GALLERY.

BY

DAVID TENIERS.

" THE artist has introduced his own portrait and that of his father ; the former, dressed in a grey coat, is seated at a table, holding a paper in his hand ; the latter, habited in black, stands at his side ; a hat and feathers hang on the back of the chair, near which is a little dog, looking at a monkey seated on a stool. Several pictures, after various masters, are placed on the ground, others cover the walls, &c., &c."

———

2 ft. by 2 ft. 6 in. C.

212.

THE FALCONER.

BY

PHILIP WOUWERMANS.

THIS excellent little picture represents an open barren scene, with a road on the right, at the side of which is a house, from whence a man is coming with a basket of vegetables; in advance of him is a gentleman on a white horse, bearing a hawk on his hand, and followed by a dog, which is on the top of a bank at the side of the road.

14 in. by 12½ in.   P.